BLAKEE
THE BALD EAGLE

Melvin Neal Edwards

Order this book online at www.trafford.com
or email orders@trafford.com

Most Trafford titles are also available at major online book retailers.

Printed in the United States of America.

ISBN: 978-1-4669-5075-7 (sc)
ISBN: 978-1-4669-5077-1 (hc)
ISBN: 978-1-4669-5076-4 (e)

Library of Congress Control Number: 2012913947

Trafford rev. 07/30/2012

 www.trafford.com

North America & international
toll-free: 1 888 232 4444 (USA & Canada)
phone: 250 383 6864 ♦ fax: 812 355 4082

THIS BOOK IS dedicated to my grandparents, John and Betsey Blake, and my mother, Edith Lorraine Blake/Edwards. This book also gives mention to old friends and family including: Mr. Jordan, Mr. Davis, Mr. Carter, Ms. White and Rochelle (who was Mr. Jordan's granddaughter), my favorite uncle Charley and my four aunts. My daughters Melicia and Christia (who made corrections and picture illustrations respectfully). Last but not least my wife's, Great Aunt Mrs. Mattie Cooper.

My grandfather, John Blake, wanted a son. The first four children born in my grandparent's household were all girls. The fifth child was a boy. The sixth child born was also a girl. This story teaches children a lesson about patience. Many times in life, we just have to wait and see what the future holds.

CHAPTER 1

———

Once upon a time, there was a Father Eagle, a Mother Eagle and six baby eagle eggs. The six baby eagle eggs were in a nest built by Father and Mother Eagle. The eagle's nest was in an old oak tree. This old oak tree was next to a large lake. The lake was called Lake Erie. Lake Erie had lots of fish swimming in its water all year round. There were big fish, little fish, and very tiny fish.

CHAPTER 2

WINTER WAS OVER and spring time was finally here. One of the six baby eagle eggs in the nest was much larger than the other five. This baby eagle egg took up most of the room in the nest. Father Eagle said to Mother Eagle "look how big this egg is! It is bigger than all of the other eggs in the nest." Mother Eagle replied "I have never seen a baby eagle egg this big! I wonder if it is going to be a girl or a boy." Father Eagle said "I know it is going to be a boy! Mother Eagle replied, "I don't know; it could be either a girl eagle or a boy eagle; we have to wait and see."

CHAPTER 3

—◦⊷◦—

As the days and weeks went by, Father and Mother Eagle were still waiting for the six eggs to hatch. Father Eagle and Mother Eagle took turns sitting softly on the six eggs to keep them warm. They would take their clawed feet and turn the eggs from top to the bottom. The large eagle egg was too hard to turn with their clawed feet. Father and Mother Eagle would take their beak and push the large baby egg to make it roll. Father Eagle excitedly said to Mother Eagle, "this baby eagle is going to be big; I know it's going to be a boy!" Mother Eagle replied "I told you, we just have to wait and see."

CHAPTER 4

E ARLY THE NEXT morning, while Father Eagle and Mother Eagle were asleep, they heard some chirping sounds coming from the eggs. Four of the small baby eagle eggs began to move from side to side. As Father and Mother Eagle closely watched the four eggs, they began hearing pecking sounds. Little by little, each of the four eggs began to break open. Moments later, the four baby eagles were out of their shells. All of the four baby eagles that hatched from their egg shells were girls. They looked just like small snow balls with black beaks, pink clawed feet and eyes tiny and black. Father and Mother Eagle were so happy.

CHAPTER 5

FATHER EAGLE SAID to Mother Eagle "I told you the small eggs would be baby girl eagles and the large egg must be a baby boy eagle! I am going to name our son after my father, BLAKE, when he is born." Mother Eagle chirped "you might be right. So far the small eggs were all baby girl eagles. What if the large egg is a girl?" Father Eagle replied "if the large eagle egg is a girl, then I am going to name her BLAKEE. BLAKEE is not the same as BLAKE, but it sounds almost the same. Anyway, I know this big egg is going to be a boy," he tweeted. Mother Eagle reminded Father Eagle time and time again "be patient and just wait and see." Mother Eagle named all of her four baby girl eagles after the letters in the alphabet. The first baby eagle girl that hatched from her egg shell was named A. The second baby girl eagle was named B; the third baby girl eagle was named C and the fourth girl was named D.

CHAPTER 6

⟶•⟨•⟩•⟵

THE FOUR BABY eagles began to make loud chirping sounds. Mother Eagle knew that her babies were hungry. Mother Eagle whistled to Father Eagle "can you go and find some food for our baby girl eagles?" Father Eagle replied "yes I will; I know just where to go to find some worms." Father Eagle soared from the nest so fast, that one of his long wings hit a branch in the tree. Mother Eagle yelled to Father Eagle "be careful" but he was already so far up in the sky. While Father Eagle went to find some food, Mother Eagle began to clean up inside the nest. There were so many egg shells lying around. One by one, Mother Eagle picked up the egg shells with her beak and flew near the bottom of the old oak tree. At the bottom of the old oak tree was a garbage can. Four times, Mother Eagle flew from the nest to the garbage can putting the hatched egg shells in it.

CHAPTER 7

MOTHER EAGLE SAT in the nest with the four baby eagles and the two baby eagle eggs. She wondered why Father Eagle was taking so long to return. As Mother Eagle looked up in the sky, she could see Father Eagle flying towards the nest. Father Eagle found lots of food for his hungry baby girl eagles. Father Eagle put all of the food next to the Mother Eagle's feet. Mother Eagle began to put small pieces of food in each of the baby eagle beak. "Sorry I took so long", chirped Father Eagle. "I stopped to tell our neighbors four of our baby eagles eggs have hatched and they were all girls. The big egg has to be a boy eagle! I also told them "we have already named him after my father BLAKE."

CHAPTER 8

ᴹOTHER EAGLE REPLIED "did you tell the
neighbors if the big egg is a girl, you are
going to name her BLAKEE?" "No" said Father Eagle.
"I know it will be a boy he declared. I never saw a baby
girl eagle egg that big. All of the big eggs were always
boy eagles." Mother Eagle squawked for the third time
to Father Eagle, "we just have to wait and see.

The very next day, Father Eagle, Mother Eagle,
and the four baby girl eagles heard a chirping sound
coming from the small eagle egg. The small eagle
egg began to move from side to side as the other
eggs had done before they hatched. Father Eagle,
Mother Eagle and the four baby girl eagles watched
the small egg as it began to break open.

CHAPTER 9

—•—

FATHER EAGLE SAID to Mother Eagle "we are about to have another baby girl eagle. This will make five eagle girls and one eagle boy." Mother Eagle did not say a word as she looked at the small egg.

As the baby eagle broke free from its egg shell, Mother and Father Eagle were so surprised. It was a baby boy eagle. Its beak was not so dark and he also looked like a small snow ball with white clawed feet. Father Eagle said to Mother Eagle "I thought for sure this small egg was going to be a girl! All small eagle eggs are always girl eagles. Mother Eagle replied "you're right; I have never seen a small boy eagle egg before. Do you want to name him after your father BLAKE?" "No", said the Father Eagle. "I want to name the big eagle egg after my father.

CHAPTER 10

L ET'S NAME THIS boy eagle after my brother Charles. I still think the big egg is going to be a boy". Mother Eagle replied "we just have to wait and see". Father Eagle said to Mother Eagle "I'll be right back; I am going to find some food for our baby boy eagle Charles." Mother Eagle replied "bring enough food for everyone; our baby eagle girls are hungry too". While Father Eagle left to find some food, Mother Eagle began to clean up the nest. Mother Eagle picked up the broken egg shell with her beak and flew to the bottom of the old oak tree. There she placed baby Charles' hatched egg shell in the garbage can. That was quick and easy

Mother Eagle, said to herself. Mother Eagle soared back to the nest to be with all of her baby eagles. So far, there were four baby girl eagles, one baby boy eagle and one large baby egg.

CHAPTER II

ᚠ

FATHER EAGLE RETURNED to the nest with plenty of food. He placed all of the food by the Mother Eagle's feet. Mother Eagle began to feed all of her baby eagles one by one. Father Eagle said to Mother Eagle, "I told all of our neighbors; the last small egg hatched was a baby boy eagle and named him Charles after my brother." Everyone was so surprised to hear that." Mother Eagle tweeted, "Is that all you said?" "No" said Father Eagle excitedly. I told them, I know the big egg will be a boy too!" Mother Eagle replied "we'll have to wait and see".

CHAPTER 12

ONE DAY, A very old man named Grandpa Jordan, and his granddaughter, Rochelle, walked by the old oak tree. Grandpa Jordan was the man who planted the tree many years ago before he moved away. He was so surprised to see how big the tree had grown. The old oak tree was so large that he could not put his arms around it. The tree was so tall; he could not see the top of it. Grandpa Jordan told his granddaughter Rochelle, "This is the acorn seed I had planted many years ago; look how big it has grown." Granddaughter Rochelle replied, "Look at all of the green leaves and big branches, I cannot count them all."

CHAPTER 13

G RANDPA JORDON LOOKED at the garbage can next to the old oak tree that he had put there many years ago. He saw the newly hatched egg shells inside of it. "Do you know what these are?" asked Grandpa Jordan. "They're egg shells Grandpa" replied Rochelle. Grandpa. Jordan said "Yes, but do you know what kind of egg shells they are?" "No" she answered. Grandpa Jordan said "these egg shells are from baby eagles; there must be an eagle's nest in this old oak tree!" Grandpa Jordan began to count the broken egg shells, "1, 2, 3, 4, and 5. There must be five baby eagles in the nest" said Grandpa Jordan. "How many baby girl eagles and baby boy eagles are there?" replied granddaughter Rochelle. Grandpa Jordon said "I don't know; you cannot tell by just looking at the baby eggs; you have to wait until they hatch to find out if it is a girl or if it is a boy.

CHAPTER 14

———

ROCHELLE TRIED TO looked up and see the eagle's nest in the old oak tree, but there were too many leaves and branches in the way. Grandpa Jordan said to Rochelle "eagles build their nest very high from the ground. The eagles nest should be at the top of the tree. Rochelle replied "I wish I could see the five baby eagles in the nest; I love birds!" Grandpa Jordan chuckled "you would need a very tall ladder to climb up the oak tree and see the eagle's nest. "Grandpa Jordan you have a very tall ladder at home!" exclaimed Rochelle. "Yes, I do, but it is too small for this old oak tree" said Grandpa Jordan. "In two more days, your school will be going to the zoo. I know the zoo will have lots of birds for you to see." Rochelle replied "I am so excited and can't wait." Grandpa Jordan said "it's time for us to go back home; it's getting late and you have school tomorrow."

CHAPTER 15

ROCHELLE REPLIED IN a loud voice as they walked away from the old oak tree "good bye eagle family!" "Do you think they heard me Grandpa?" "I believe they did hear you Rochelle" said Grandpa.

CHAPTER 16

E ASTER VACATION FROM school was going to start in two days. Every year, all of the schools in the district would go on a field trip to the local zoo before Good Friday. All of the students were so excited and happy about going to the zoo. Rochelle's birthday was on that Thursday, and there was going to be a big surprise party for her at the zoo. Rochelle was going to be eight years old. Everyone knew about the surprise birthday party for Rochelle and did not tell her. There was going to be a cake, ice cream, balloons, birthday hats, juice and pizza for all of Rochelle's friends and teachers. There was also going to be an Easter egg hunt, prizes and pony rides. The surprise birthday party for Rochelle at the zoo was going to be next to the red, white and blue bird house building. Everyone knew that Rochelle loved birds. Rochelle's mom, dad, grandma and Grandpa Jordan were excited about the surprise party.

CHAPTER 17

THE NEXT DAY, Rochelle looked so sad when she came home from school. Rochelle's mom, dad, grandma and Grandpa Jordon all asked "why do you look so sad Rochelle?" Rochelle replied "Miss White my teacher told all of the students at school today the big red, white and blue bird house building at the zoo was closed. The zoo keepers could not find any birds this year for the bird house building. "There will be lots of other animals to see at the zoo tomorrow", said Grandpa Jordan. "I know." "I just wanted to go inside the big bird house building to see some birds; I love birds" she said. Rochelle's mom, dad, grandma and Grandpa Jordan said "don't worry Rochelle, everything will be alright; you just wait and see." Rochelle walked slowly to her room to do her homework. Rochelle looked out of her window and did not see or hear any birds. "I miss my bird friends" said Rochelle.

CHAPTER 18

―――

WHILE ROCHELLE WAS in her room feeling very sad, Grandpa Jordan had a great idea. Grandpa Jordan said to Rochelle's mom, dad and grandma "I know where to find some birds for the big bird house building. There is an eagle family that has built its nest in the old oak tree I planted years ago. I counted five baby eagle egg shells from the garbage can next to the tree. The big bird house building at the zoo will be a nice home for this eagle family." Rochelle's mom, dad and grandma were so happy to hear about this great news. Grandpa Jordan said "I am going to visit my two old friends Mr. Davis and Mr. Carter and ask them for their help!" Mr. Davis is the fire chief and has a big fire truck with a long ladder to reach the top of the old oak tree. Mr. Carter is the zoo keeper that takes care of all the animals at the zoo".

CHAPTER 19

———

WHILE GRANDPA JORDAN left the house to visit his two old friends, Rochelle came from her room. "Where is Grandpa Jordan?" said Rochelle to her mom, dad and grandma. They replied "Grandpa Jordan went to help a family move into a new home." Rochelle's mom said "it's going to be some ones birthday tomorrow; I wonder whose it will be?" Rochelle, with a big smile on her face sang "it's going to be my birthday!" Rochelle's mom, dad and Grandma all asked "if she was excited about her eighth birthday." "Yes I am, but I really wanted to see birds at the zoo tomorrow" Rochelle sadly replied. Rochelle's mom, dad and grandma said "everything will be alright; just wait and see."

CHAPTER 20

GRANDPA JORDAN WENT to see his two old friends Mr. Davis the fire chief and Mr. Carter the zoo keeper. Mr. Davis and Mr. Carter lived next door to each other. Grandpa Jordan saw both Mr. Davis the fire chief and Mr. Carter the zoo keeper standing outside of their house talking to each other. "Hello" said Grandpa Jordan, as he was getting out of his blue truck. "Hello" replied both Mr. Davis and Mr. Carter to Grandpa Jordan. All of them walked towards each other and shook hands in excitement. "We have not seen you in years! How are you?" Grandpa Jordan said "I am fine; it has been over five years since we last saw each other. I am in town because of my granddaughter Rochelle's surprise birthday party at the zoo tomorrow, and I need both of your help."

CHAPTER 21

GRANDPA JORDAN SAID "I heard the big red, white and blue bird building at the zoo is closed". Mr. Carter the zoo keeper replied "yes it is closed. We could not find any birds this year." Grandpa Jordan said "I know where there is a nice eagle family with five baby eagles. The bird house building at the zoo would be a perfect home for this young eagle family." Mr. Carter the zoo keeper was so happy to hear this good news. Mr. Carter the zoo keeper asked "where can I find this eagle family?" Grandpa Jordan said "this eagle family built a nest in the old oak tree I planted years ago next to the lake." Mr. Carter the zoo keeper questioned "do you know how many baby girl eagles and baby boy eagles there are?" "No" said Grandpa Jordan. "I only saw the newly hatched eagle eggs shells in the garbage can next to the old oak tree."

CHAPTER 22

"How can I help?" asked Mr. Davis the fire chief. "You have the big red fire truck with the very long ladder to reach the top of the old oak tree" explained Grandpa Jordan. The eagle's nest is somewhere near the top of the tree. I would like to move the eagle family into the big red, white and blue bird house today so that it will be opened tomorrow for my granddaughter Rochelle's surprise birthday party." Mr. Davis the fire chief and Mr. Carter the zoo keeper both said to their old friend grandpa Jordan "that sounds like a great idea!"

CHAPTER 23

M R. CARTER SAID "I'm going to the zoo to open up the big red, white and blue bird house building. I will get everything ready for the young eagle family." Mr. Davis the fire chief said "I'm going to the fire hall to get the big red fire truck with the long ladder. I will bring it to the old oak tree by the lake." Grandpa Jordan replied in an excited voice "I will meet you at the old oak tree" to Mr. Davis the fire chief and "I will see you at the zoo" to Mr. Carter.

CHAPTER 24

M R. DAVIS THE fire chief came to the old oak tree by the lake with all of his fire fighters workers. There were three big red fire engine trucks. Grandpa Jordan was so surprise to see all of the other fire fighters and fire trucks. Grandpa Jordan said to Mr. Davis the fire chief "I thought you were going to come here by yourself". Mr. Davis the fire chief replied "oh no; all fire fighters always work as a team; we never work alone. We always work together and help each other. We help other people too."

CHAPTER 25

THERE WERE SO many people who came near the old oak tree when they saw the three big red fire engine trucks and fire fighters. Everyone wondered what was going on. Some people thought there was a cat caught in the tree that could not get down. Everyone came near to see what was happening. Mr. Davis the fire chief and the fire fighter workers made everyone stand back at a safe distance. Even Grandpa Jordan had to stand back from the old oak tree. Mr. Davis the fire chief told everyone "the fire department is here to take an eagle family from the old oak tree and bring them to a nice new home."

CHAPTER 26

T HE FIRE FIGHTERS raised their ladders to reach the top of the old oak tree. Each fire fighter wore special gloves to protect their hands from the eagle's sharp claws. As the fire fighters climbed their ladders, they saw the eagle's nest at the top of the tree. The fire fighters saw the mother eagle, the father eagle, the five baby eagles and the big baby eagle egg. One of the fire fighters called Mr. Davis the fire chief from the special walkie talkie radios each fire fighter wears and said "chief, we found the eagle's nest; there is a mother eagle, father eagle, five baby eagles and one big baby eagle egg that has not hatched yet." Mr. Davis the fire chief replied "tell everyone to take their time bringing the birds down from the tree and to be careful with the big baby eagle egg."

CHAPTER 27

M R. DAVIS THE fire chief could not wait to tell Grandpa Jordan the good news. Mr. Davis walked over to where Grandpa Jordan was standing and said "you were right! My fire fighters found the eagle's nest at the top of the tree. They saw the father eagle, the mother eagle, five baby eagles and one big baby eagle egg that have not yet hatched." Grandpa Jordan replied "that's great news. I knew there were five baby eagles, but I did not know about the big baby eagle egg."

CHAPTER 28

THE FIRE FIGHTERS took their time bringing down each and every eagle bird from the ladder. They also were very careful with the big baby eagle egg. All of the eagles and the big baby eagle egg were placed in a special box inside of the big red fire truck. Grandpa Jordan saw each of the baby eagle birds before they were put in the fire truck. Grandpa Jordan said to Mr. Davis the fire chief "it looks like there are four baby girl eagles and one baby boy eagle". Mr. Davis, the fire chief replied "what do you think the big egg will be?" Grandpa Jordan said "I don't know; you cannot tell by just looking at the egg. You have to wait and see when it hatches." All of the people standing near the old oak tree were happy and excited to see the eagle family. They also saw how well the fire fighters worked together as a team.

CHAPTER 29

M R. DAVIS THE fire chief and all of the fire fighters sat in the red fire truck. They were on their way to the zoo to bring the eagle family to their new home. Mr. Davis the fire chief, told Grandpa Jordan to sit next to him in the fire engine truck. Grandpa Jordan was so excited because he had always wanted to sit in a fire truck.

CHAPTER 30

WHEN THEY ARRIVED at the zoo, Mr. Carter the zoo keeper was so surprise to see the three big red fire trucks and all of the fire fighters. Mr. Carter was also surprised to see Grandpa Jordan sitting next to Mr. Davis the fire chief in one of the fire trucks. Mr. Carter the zoo keeper was told about the mother eagle, the father eagle, the four baby girl eagles, the baby boy eagle boy and the big eagle egg. Grandpa Jordan and Mr. Davis the fire chief were also surprised to see so many zoo keeper workers helping at the big red, white and blue bird house building. The zoo keepers and the fire fighters worked as one big team. It only took ten minutes to put the eagle family into their new home.

CHAPTER 31

THE BIG EAGLE egg was placed in the front of a thick glass wall for all to see with the five baby eagles. Mother Eagle and Father Eagle were also put there. There were lots of food, water and flying room. After all that was said and done, everyone shook hands in doing a great job. The bird house was going to be opened tomorrow.

CHAPTER 32

April 19th was finally here. It was the last day of school before Easter break and it was also Rochelle's eighth birthday. All of the students were told by their teachers not to bring any books to school. Everyone was going on the field trip to the zoo. Rochelle was still a little sad about the big bird house being closed, but she had a smile on her face because it was her birthday. Rochelle could not wait to go to school today because of the field trip to the zoo. She always had a good time on field trips. Rochelle's mom, dad, grandma and Grandpa Jordan all said happy birthday to her. Rochelle's mom made Rochelle a very nice birthday hat to wear to school. Rochelle gave her mom, dad, grandma and Grandpa Jordan a hug and a kiss before she went to school. "Enjoy your day at the zoo and remember everything will be alright," said Grandpa Jordan to Rochelle.

CHAPTER 33

A LL OF THE students were told to report to the lunch room. Mrs. M. Cooper the principal told all of the students to be on their best behavior at the zoo. She also told the teachers to make sure each student had a name tag on their shirt. Each student was given a bag of candy. Inside the bag of candy were jelly beans and a small chocolate covered bunny rabbit. Mrs. M. Cooper the principal wished all of the students and teachers a happy Easter before they left for the zoo.

CHAPTER 34

THE SCHOOL BUSES were lined up in front of the school ready for the big day at the zoo. The teachers made sure each student had a name tag on as Mrs. M. Cooper the principal said. All of the students were told to go on the school bus with their teacher. The bus drivers reminded the children not to eat on the school bus. Rochelle was the only student on the bus with a birthday hat. Everyone knew about the surprise birthday party for Rochelle at the zoo. No one said a word to Rochelle about the big surprise. The zoo was about ten minutes away from the school. It was a short bus ride. All of the students were so surprised and happy to see the big sign in front of the zoo. The big sign in front of the zoo read THE BIRD HOUSE IS OPENED.

CHAPTER 35

ROCHELLE WAS SO excited about the good news that she did a little wiggle dance in her bus seat and clapped her hands. Rochelle loved birds. Miss White and all the teachers were also surprised. The day before, Miss White and all the teachers told the students the big bird house would be closed. All of the students could not wait to get off of the school bus and go inside of the zoo. The teachers reminded the children to be on their best behavior, as Mrs. M. Cooper the principal had said.

CHAPTER 36

ROCHELLE ASKED HER teacher Miss White if her class could go to the big bird house first. Miss White knew that the surprise birthday party for Rochelle was going to be at 12:00 noon near the bird house. It was only 9:10am. Miss White said to Rochelle and her other students "we are going to see the other animals first, and go to the big bird house last." The teachers and students saw all kinds of animals at the zoo. There were lions, tigers and bears. Some of the students said "oh my!"

CHAPTER 37

I T WAS ALMOST noon. Miss White and her students were going to the big bird house. This was the moment Rochelle had been waiting for! Rochelle was so excited that she moved to the front of the line and walked with Miss White, her teacher. When Miss White and her class went inside the big bird house, they saw the eagle family. Everyone saw the mother eagle, the father eagle, the five baby eagles and the big eagle egg. Mr. Carter the zoo keeper told all of the children that this eagle family was found in an old oak tree near Lake Erie. Rochelle was so excited she screamed, "that is the tree my Grandpa Jordan planted years ago!"

CHAPTER 38

MR. CARTER THE zoo keeper decided to take father eagle outside because there were too many teachers, students, parents and children in the big bird house. Mr. Carter the zoo keeper wore special gloves to protect his hands and arms from the sharp claws of father eagle. Rochelle was so happy and excited to see father eagle up close. Mr. Carter the zoo keeper showed all of the students father eagle's long wings. He called it the eagles' wingspan. Mr. Carter the zoo keeper told the students that eagles have very good eye sight and they build their nest in large trees near rivers. All of the students were excited to see and hear about the eagles.

CHAPTER 39

WHILE ROCHELLE WAS looking at father eagle, Mr. Carter the zoo keeper pointed his finger and told Rochelle to look behind her. When Rochelle turned around, her friends, classmates, teachers, Mrs. M. Cooper the principal, her mom, dad, grandma, Grandpa Jordan, Mr. Davis the fire chief, firemen, fire women, bus drivers and all of the zoo keepers said "surprise and happy birthday to Rochelle." Rochelle was so surprised that she put her hand up to her mouth. Everyone sang happy birthday to Rochelle. Rochelle had so many presents. There was pizza, juice, cake, ice cream, jelly beans and chocolate cover easter bunny candy. All of the students wore a birthday hat and was given a balloon. There was a big Easter egg hunt, pony rides and all of the students were given a chance to sit in the big fire trucks.

CHAPTER 40

WHILE EVERYONE WAS having a good time at Rochelle's birthday party, Mr. Carter the zoo keeper said in a loud and excited voice "come to the bird house! the big eagle egg is about to hatch! Everyone at Rochelle's birthday party hurried to the big bird house to see. The big eagle egg was moving from side to side. Everyone heard pecking noises and then the big egg started to break open. Soon the baby eagle was out of its shell. It was a beautiful baby girl eagle.

CHAPTER 41

T HE BABY GIRL eagle looked like a snow ball with a nice looking beak and pink clawed feet. Father Eagle chirped "her name is BLAKEE!" Mother Eagle tweeted "because BLAKEE four sisters were named A, B, C, and D, BLAKEE's first name will be the letter E". So Mother Eagle took the last letter from BLAKEE and her name became E BLAKE. There was a sign placed next to the glass wall which read "Baby Eagle Girl E Blake Born on April 19th."

CHAPTER 42

W HEN ROCHELLE RETURNED home from the field trip, she told her mom, dad, grandma and Grandpa Jordan that was the best birthday she ever had. Rochelle said to Grandma Jordan "you were right; everything worked out fine!" Grandma Jordan replied "it sure did, all is well and it ends well!"

CHAPTER 43

MEANWHILE, BACK AT the zoo, when all of the animals were put back in their cages, the zoo keepers went home and all of the lights were turn off, Father Eagle said to Mother Eagle "I really thought BLAKEE was going to be a boy." Mother Eagle replied "I told you, we had to wait and see!" Father Eagle said "I learned a good lesson today!" Mother Eagle replied "what good lesson did you learn?" Father Eagle said "I will never count my eagles before they hatch!"

THE END

CPSIA information can be obtained at www.ICGtesting.com
Printed in the USA
BVOW011758140812

297870BV00001B/51/P